Dog Days

Becky Citra

ORCA BOOK PUBLISHERS

Copyright © 2003 Becky Citra

National Library of Canada Cataloguing in Publication Data
Citra, Becky

Dog days / Becky Citra.

"An Orca young reader"

ISBN 1-55143-256-0

I. Title.

PS8555.I87D63 2003   jC813'.54   C2002-911517-5

PZ7.C499Do 2003

Library of Congress Control Number: 2002115955

Summary: Brady must overcome his fear of dogs if he wants to make friends in a new town.

Free teachers' guide available.

Orca Book Publishers gratefully acknowledges the support of its publishing programs provided by the following agencies: the Department of Canadian Heritage, the Canada Council for the Arts, and the British Columbia Arts Council.

Cover design by Christine Toller
Cover & interior illustrations by Helen Flook

Printed and bound in Canada

IN CANADA	IN THE UNITED STATES
Orca Book Publishers	Orca Book Publishers
1030 North Park Street	PO Box 468
Victoria, BC Canada	Custer, WA USA
V8T 1C6	98240-0468

05 04 03 • 5 4 3 2 1

chapter one

"We are now approaching the planet Jupiter."

Brady piloted his model of the Starship *Enterprize* across Gramp's living room. He dodged between an ancient windup record player and an old dusty saddle.

The model was an early birthday present from Mom. He'd stayed up late three nights building it. Brady bit his lip. It was one of the best things he'd ever made, and there was no one to see it.

Footsteps slapped in the hall. Brady

landed the Starship gently on a faded velvet armchair. Gramp shuffled into the living room. His slippers looked like bear paws. Wild horses galloped across his pajamas. He was carrying a large box wrapped in newspaper.

Mom came through the kitchen doorway, wiping her hands on a tea towel. She shot Brady a warning look. Brady knew what it meant. Pretend you like the present. His heart thumped. Gramp always gave him weird presents. Last year it was a horseshoe. Mom had told him to hang it over his door for good luck. Well, it sure hadn't worked.

For a second, Brady let himself think about last year's birthday. He and Mom had been living in the city, far away from Gramp. The horseshoe had come in the mail in a box covered with masking tape. Brady and his best friends, Thomas and Jason, had rolled their eyes and laughed. Then Mom had treated them to the pool and the arcade and a movie. It had been a great birthday. He'd planned to do exactly the same thing this year.

That was before Gramp got his

problem. That's what Mom called it. Gramp's problem. Anger bubbled up inside Brady again.

"He's afraid to go out of the house," Mom had explained patiently. "It's sort of an old person's thing."

"Mr. Tadley goes out, and he's old," Brady had pointed out. Mr. Tadley lived in the apartment next to Mom and Brady. He rode a motorcycle and gave Brady a loonie when they rode up in the elevator.

Mom's forehead had wrinkled. That was a bad sign. Brady should have seen trouble coming. But it was hard to worry about a grandfather he had never even met, a grandfather who lived thousands of miles away in a little town on the other side of the country.

Then Mom had ruined his life.

"Moving? We're moving?" Brady's stomach had plunged to his feet.

Cold with shock, he had listened to Mom's arguments. She had a great new job opportunity. They could see Gramp every day. It would be super to get out of the city. They'd try it for a year and then decide.

"We could even think about getting a dog," she had suggested. "Kids in small towns have dogs. It could help you get over your nervousness."

Brady had shot her an icy look. "How many times do I have to tell you? I'm not nervous of dogs. I just don't like them."

Just because Brady crossed the street when a dog approached and once said he approved of the No Dogs rule in their apartment building, Mom thought he was afraid of dogs. She blamed it on what she called his *bad experience*. When he was three years old, a friend's Saint Bernard had cornered him in a bathroom and he'd been trapped for two hours before anyone noticed. Brady sighed. Everyone acted like it was against the law if you didn't think dogs were the greatest thing in the world.

Beside him, Gramp coughed. Brady shifted his thoughts back to the box. Gramp's bright eyes bored into him. He tore the newspaper off in long strips and crumpled it into a wad. Cautiously he lifted the lid of the box.

"Boots," he said in disbelief.

The boots had high heels, pointy toes and scrolly designs on the sides. Dust lined the creases in the leather, and something crusty and brown stuck to the soles.

"My old boots, when I was a boy!" said Gramp. He stared defiantly at Brady. "That's horse manure!"

Brady shuddered. Gramp used to be a cowboy. He'd ridden wild horses. He'd been a champion roper in the rodeos. Ever since they moved here, Brady had heard the stories. That didn't mean Brady wanted to be a cowboy too. He had a sickening feeling Mom would try to make him wear this stuff.

"They look like girl's boots," he muttered.

Mom frowned.

Brady sighed. "Thanks anyway, Gramp."

"Ha!" said Gramp. He shot Brady a long hard look. Then he sidled towards the card table by the window. Brady's chest tightened. He knew what was coming next.

Every afternoon Mom and Brady rode their bikes the six blocks from their new house to Gramp's house to check on him and make his supper. Brady always got stuck playing cards with Gramp. The trouble was, Brady was the world's worst card player. He mixed up spades and clubs. And he couldn't shuffle.

"I'm going upstairs to read comics," he said quickly. He caught Mom's eye. "Just for a little while."

Gramp collected old Marvel comics. He stored them in cardboard boxes in a little room at the top of the house. Brady had discovered them a week ago.

The stairs in Gramp's house were narrow and dark. *Ooomph.* Brady tripped over something heavy lurking in the shadows. A low growl rumbled in the darkness.

Brady's heart jumped into his throat. "Hey, look out, Grit!"

Grit was Gramp's dog. His name was short for True Grit. In dog years, Grit was as old as Gramp. He had black-and-white fur, a rusty patch between his ears and washy eyes. On the wall in Gramp's living room was a photograph of Grit in a gold frame, a much younger looking Grit, with a glossy coat and bright eyes, clutching a Frisbee in his mouth and with a red ribbon hanging around his neck.

"Frisbee-catching champion," Gramp had boasted when he caught Brady looking at the picture. He'd rummaged around on a shelf and produced a blue-and-red Frisbee. He rubbed off the dust with his sleeve. "This was his favorite."

For just a second, Brady had pictured himself throwing the Frisbee for the big black dog. He'd take him down to that park near their new house. A group of guys hung out there with a bunch of dogs, throwing sticks for the dogs and tossing a ball around. Brady had been watching them for almost three weeks. He'd biked past lots of time slowly, but he couldn't get up the nerve to say hi.

"Six years in a row," Gramp said, giving Brady a sly look.

Brady had shrugged and pretended

not to be interested. The one time he had tried to pat Grit, the dog had growled and showed his teeth, which only confirmed what Brady already knew. It was safer to leave dogs alone.

Brady lifted his foot to step over Grit's head. Carefully.

Grit growled again, a deep menacing growl.

Brady gulped. "What? Do you think you own the stairs?" He tried to sound brave. Dogs can smell your fear. But his voice squeaked on the word "stairs."

Grit lowered his head and closed his eyes. Brady chewed his lip. Grit was a pro at trying to fake you out. He'd wait until you thought he was sleeping and then SNAP!

Brady thought about Gramp skulking around downstairs with the deck of cards. He thought about shuffling. He swallowed hard, took a deep breath and leaped over the dog.

Rrrrumph, grumbled Grit, his eyes yellow slits.

"Ha!" shouted Brady from the safety of the top stair. "You should do something about your dog breath!"

Brady went into the room at the end of the hall. It had a low slanted ceiling and one window. Cardboard boxes covered the floor. Brady had poked through most of them, digging through old books, dusty blue and green bottles, dog show ribbons, pieces of horse harnesses, boots, odd-shaped pieces of metal, tools, wood scraps, batteries and even a box crammed with decks of playing cards.

Mom and Gramp argued about Gramp's junk almost every day. Secretly, Brady thought it was the only good thing about coming here. In the back of his mind, he was thinking about building a space station. Lots of Gramp's stuff would be great for that.

The comic books filled three boxes. He had cleared a place on the floor for reading. Now he stretched out on his stomach and flipped through a thick Superman comic. He tried to read slowly. If he was careful, he could make Gramp's comics last for the rest of this boring summer.

The most boring summer in his whole life.

Probably the most boring summer in the century.

The most boring summer in the millennium. A sudden lump filled Brady's throat. He and Jason and Thomas liked to say things like that. They could go on forever, until they drove everyone around them crazy.

Brady flopped onto his back and closed his eyes. He thought about the guys in the park. Three boys who looked like they'd be in grade five, like him, had been there this morning. It had been hot already by ten o'clock, and the dogs were swimming after sticks in the creek. Brady had stopped in a shady spot and watched.

Brady remembered what Mom had said. Kids in small towns have dogs. He sighed. They should have moved to Jupiter. He was pretty sure there were no dogs there.

After a while he got up and went to the window. He pushed it open and leaned on the sill.

At the bottom of Gramp's yard was an old garage, half buried in thistles, used tires and garden tools. Gramp kept it locked with a rusty padlock. Brady had peered through the small window on the side lots of times, but it was cracked and thick with dust.

The garage was probably full of neat old junk that he could use for his space station. Brady sighed. He would love one look inside the garage, just one look.

He ran his finger along the dust on the windowsill. A movement caught his eye. An orange cat stalked across the moss-covered roof of the garage. The cat jumped to the ground. It arched its back and melted through a thin black crack along the edge of the door.

Brady blinked. He leaned farther out the window.

Either the cat was Houdini or... Gramp had left the garage door open.

Suddenly, this birthday was getting a little bit better. Brady took a big breath. If he tiptoed, he could sneak outside without anyone noticing. He turned to leave the room.

A low growl sent prickles up his spine. In the shadowy hallway, a pair of white fangs gleamed.

Grit was blocking the doorway.

chapter two

Grrrrrrr, rumbled Grit.

The back of Brady's neck prickled. He slid his eyes away from Grit
and stuck his head out the window.
It opened onto a narrow strip of shin-
gled roof. A metal drainpipe stuck up
at the end: his escape route.

Brady licked his lips. Guys did things
like that in books. Not in real life.

He peeked over his shoulder. Grit
stared at him, his yellow eyes unblinking.
A thin thread of saliva hung from the
corner of his mouth. He yawned, showing
a mouthful of deadly looking teeth. With

a grunt, he flopped down on his stomach. His eyes never left Brady.

Brady made up his mind. He scrambled through the window and squatted on the shingles. He kept one arm hooked over the windowsill. It was as hot as a furnace on the roof.

The houses on Gramp's street were close together. They had neatly mowed lawns and picket fences. All but Gramp's. A rusty barbed wire fence surrounded Gramp's yard. The grass was long and brownish. Gramp called it his hayfield. Mom said if Gramp didn't let her cut it soon, the man from City Hall would complain.

Brady looked at the grass with interest. The City Hall man was probably due any day now. Too bad. The hayfield was one of the few things he and Gramp agreed on. It was a great place for building forts or pretending you were an explorer. You could get lost in Gramp's hayfield for days.

Laundry fluttered on the clothesline at the yellow house next door. A woman opened an upstairs window and shook out a cloth. The people had been away since the beginning of the summer, but they must have got back last night.

Brady took a deep breath and inched along the roof. A shingle broke loose and clattered over the edge. He gulped and fixed his eyes on the piece of drainpipe sticking up at the end. He'd be okay if he didn't look straight down.

Brady looked. Just one peek. Down. Way down. Into the tall grass of Gramp's hayfield. A wave of dizziness swept over him. The hayfield swirled into a brown blur. His stomach lurched. He pressed up against the side of the house, closed his eyes and counted to ten.

A heavy thud interrupted his counting. He opened his eyes and looked back. Grit's two front paws rested on the windowsill. His eyes blinked in the bright sun. When he saw Brady, a low growl rumbled in his throat.

With a yelp, Brady scuttled on his hands and knees the rest of the way. He grabbed the top of the drainpipe with both hands. His heart thumping wildly, he slid his legs over the edge and wrapped them around the drain-pipe.

Roooo, howled Grit.

Brady closed his eyes again. The drainpipe slipped through his sweaty hands. Halfway down he heard a rip-ping sound. He felt himself swing out into the air. He landed with a thump on his back.

For one whole minute Brady thought he was dead. Then he wiggled his toes. He wiggled his fingers. Slowly he sat up. He pushed the piece of broken drainpipe off his legs.

He had made it! Brady glanced nervously at the house. The vacuum cleaner roared from the living room. A wide grin spread across his face. He raced through the long grass to the old garage.

The garage door creaked when he pulled it. For a second Brady froze. He looked back at the house again. Then he slipped inside.

Pale light filtered through the dusty

window, but he couldn't see much. Just a big black shape in the shadows. Brady opened the door wider, letting in a shaft of sunlight. It gleamed on shining chrome and metallic red paint.

"Wow," said Brady softly.

A monster truck sat high up in the air on huge tires. A big black "67" was painted boldly on the door. Golden lightning bolts zigzagged along the sides. Across the hood, in red-and-orange letters that looked like flames, flashed the words Desert Racer.

Desert Racer. Wow. A truck like this could go anywhere. Brady's heart thumped. How could Gramp have kept this a secret?

Brady opened the door and slid onto the seat. The truck was open at the front with no windshield. He gripped the steering wheel and pressed his back into the seat. Hot wind blew against his face. The crowd roared.

Brady licked his lips. He'd give anything, *anything*, for a ride in Desert Racer.

A shadow fell across his face. A voice

said, "Hey! Cool truck."

Brady spun sideways. A witch stood in the doorway. Brady blinked. The witch stepped inside. She was just a girl, a girl with a black hat and green hair.

The girl smiled. "I'm Abra. I live next door. We heard you were coming."

"Oh," said Brady. He stared at her. She looked weird.

"Does your grandfather ever drive this thing?"

"Of course," said Brady stiffly. He didn't want to admit that he didn't have a clue. "But no one except Gramp and me are supposed to know about it," he added quickly, "so don't go telling people."

Abra shrugged. "Sure."

Brady climbed out of the truck. He had a wild hope that Gramp would leave the garage door open from now on. He could sit in Desert Racer whenever he came to visit.

"Come on," he said to Abra.

Brady closed the door carefully behind them. The open padlock dangled on the latch. For a second Brady considered slipping it into his pocket. But

Gramp might get suspicious.

"Aren't you going to lock it?" said Abra.

"No."

Abra flicked a piece of her green hair. "How come you were on the roof?"

Brady looked startled. She asked a lot of questions. He said in a low voice, "I was locked in the attic. Without oxygen. And an alien was guarding the staircase!"

Abra tilted her head and gave him a long hard look. Her eyes were green, like her hair. Brady sighed. It was just his luck that a girl lived next door. A weird girl.

On Jupiter there were probably no girls. And no dogs.

And then Brady froze. A movement in the middle of Gramp's hayfield had caught his eye. The day was hot and windless, but the tall grass was moving.

Brady stared harder. Something was creeping through Gramp's hayfield. It rippled through the grass like a snake, and it was heading right towards him.

chapter three

Brady stood very still, his eyes riveted on the swaying, shimmering grass.

He caught a glimpse of golden fur. Two eyes glinted in the sun.

Brady's heart gave a sudden lurch in his chest. "Look out!" he yelled.

WHOOSH! Something big and furry and heavy crashed against his stomach.

Brady fell over backwards. He lay sprawled on the hard ground. A wet tongue slopped across his arm. A dog!

"Cool It, come here!" shouted Abra. She was laughing. She grabbed the dog's collar and looked at Brady, who stood up, wiping his hands across his face. "He always sneaks up on people. Sorry."

Brady glared at Abra. "You never said you had a dog." He brushed dirt off his jeans. His legs felt like porridge.

"You never asked."

Brady licked his lips. He couldn't stop staring at Cool It. His thick fur was golden in the sun. His eyes danced. He slapped his long plumed tail back and forth against Abra's legs.

"I was actually going to walk to Reptile Rage," said Abra. "Then I saw you on the roof. Cool It needs a new collar. Do you want to come?"

Reptile Rage was only three blocks away. It was the best pet store Brady had ever seen. The owner, Dextra, let kids hold the snakes and pet the iguanas. Once Brady had cleaned the boa constrictor's cage all by himself.

"Are you taking Cool It?" asked Brady.

"Sure."

"Are you wearing that witch's hat?"

Abra gave him a hard look.

Brady sighed. This is what happened when you were desperate. You agreed to go for a walk with a girl with a huge, out-of-control dog. "I'll come. Just wait a sec while I tell Mom."

He looked at Abra's face. He didn't want her to get the wrong idea. "But after that, I'm going to be busy."

A blue awning stretched over the door of the pet store. A sleepy-eyed tortoise blinked in the wide front window. A bunch of kids huddled around a poster stuck on the brick wall. Brady recognized two of the guys from the park. They were talking in loud voices.

"Hi, Abra. Hi, Cool It," said a girl. She had masses of skinny brown braids and a row of earrings in each ear.

"Hi, Julia. Hi, guys. This is Brady. He just moved here a while ago."

A few of the kids glanced at Brady. The rest kept staring at the poster.

DOG SHOW
Where? Reptile Rage parking lot
When? Friday morning, July 26
!!!!!!!!RIBBONS!!!!!!!!
Best-behaved dog, funniest dog,
biggest dog and more.

"That only gives me four days to train Cool It," said Abra. She chewed her bottom lip.

"I'm definitely bringing my dog," said Julia. "She's a Lhasa Apso. She'll definitely win rarest dog."

"I'm bringing Butch," said a boy with spiky blond hair. He smirked. "He's been to obedience classes."

Brady's chest tightened.

Is that all anyone thought about in this stupid town? Dogs?

Brady's cheeks burned. He was probably the only kid in the whole town without a dog. In the whole world.

"Are you going in the show?" said Julia.

"What?" Brady blinked. She was talking to him. And now everyone was looking.

Julia tossed her braids. "Do you have a dog?"

"Uh...sort of," Brady mumbled. He took a big breath. "My grandfather and I...uh...share a dog."

"Grit," said Abra. "He was a Frisbee-catching champion."

Everyone looked interested now. For the first time, they were really noticing Brady. Brady licked his lips.

"Six times," he said weakly.

"Neat," said a boy.

For one whole second Brady felt great. Then panic flooded him. What was he doing? He had said he shared Gramp's dog! He opened his mouth to take it back, but it was too late. The kids were wandering away, talking loudly about the show.

"We could train together," said Abra.

"I don't think so," said Brady quickly. His stomach felt hollow. His lips were dry.

Maybe the kids would forget.

Fat chance.

They thought he was the owner of a six-time Frisbee-champion wonder dog.

Brady groaned. He knew they should have moved to Jupiter.

chapter four

Brady squatted by the kitchen table. He waved the red-and-blue Frisbee in front of Grit's nose. "Come on, Grit. Remember how much fun it used to be."

Grit's ears twitched.

"Six-time champion. You were the best, Grit. Come on, you can do it."

Grit slunk forward on his belly. He sniffed the Frisbee. For a second a spark of interest flickered in his old eyes. Then he heaved a huge sigh and flopped his head down on the floor.

Brady glared at him. "What are you doing?"

He waited for a minute. Grit was falling asleep.

Brady took a big breath. He leaned forward and touched Grit's neck. Gently.

Nothing happened.

Brady felt himself relax. Of course nothing happened. After all, Gramp patted Grit all the time, and Grit just wagged his tail.

Slowly Brady slipped his fingers under the edge of the red bandana that was tied around Grit's neck.

He counted to five. Then he tugged.

Grit rumbled like a train deep in his throat.

Brady yanked his hand away. Beads of sweat broke out on his forehead.

He took a shaky breath. It wasn't going to work. He was risking his life, and he couldn't get Grit to budge from under the table. How was he ever going to drag him all the way to a stupid dog show?

Brady thought about the kids at Reptile Rage. He thought about the boy from the park who had looked right at him and said, "Neat."

Brady went into the living room. Mom was flapping a dust cloth over the furniture. She stepped over Gramp's collection of old syrup cans and around his five broken TVs. Her mouth was clamped shut in a tight line.

Gramp sat hunched over a table by the window, dealing cards. He leered at Brady. Brady sighed. Might as well get it over with.

"Crazy Eights," shouted Gramp. "Best of ten." Brady opened his mouth to protest. Grit padded into the room. His toenails click-clicked on the floor. He flopped under the table with a grunt and rested his head on Gramp's bear-paw slipper.

"You really should take that dog out more," said Brady. "It's not healthy to let him sleep all the time."

Gramp slapped an ace of spades onto the table. "Come on, boy! I'll give you a run for your money."

Brady slumped down in his chair and stared gloomily at his cards. "I could buy a leash at the pet store," he said hopefully. "You know, take Grit for some walks."

"The game, boy!" bellowed Gramp.

"Brady, the name is Brady," Brady muttered. He laid his queen of clubs on the ace of spades.

"That's a club!" shrieked Gramp. "In Crazy Eights, you have to play the same suit. Unless you have an eight!"

"I *know* that." Brady's stomach shriveled. Wait until Gramp saw him shuffle. He'd tried to practice, but he was getting worse, not better.

Gramp cleaned him in the first game. And the second. And the third.

Ten games. Skunked.

Gramp rubbed his hands through his hair. It stood up in fuzzy gray tufts. His cheeks were pink with excitement. He peered slyly at Brady.

Brady shrugged. "I don't care," he said. But he did. Just once he would love to beat Gramp.

"Skunked him, mother," said Gramp.

"Mmm," said Mom. She sank down on the couch. A dust ball clung to her eyebrow. "I don't understand what these housekeepers I get for you *do* all day."

Gramp stuck out his chin. Brady smiled. He was saved. Mom could argue forever about messy rooms. He slid off his chair and pulled back the curtain.

Abra and Julia were parading up and down the sidewalk in front of Gramp's house. Cool It tugged on the end of a leash. A small white mop of a dog bobbed at Julia's side. Brady could hear the girls yelling things like "Heel!" and "Stay!"

His stomach flipped over. He let the curtain drop. Maybe he could go to Jupiter on the day of the dog show.

Gramp had slid lower in his chair. Mom was charging full steam ahead. "I can't believe the mess you're in. What on earth did Mrs. Short do when she was here?"

Mrs. Short was Gramp's last housekeeper. Brady had heard all about her. She'd quit just before Brady and Mom moved to Gramp's town.

Gramp shot a triumphant look at Brady. "She played cards."

No wonder she quit, thought Brady. He wondered who Mom would find next.

"Honestly, Dad! I start my new job tomorrow, and I'm not going to have time to deal with this."

Gramp closed his eyes. Grit moaned and rolled onto his back. He churned his legs in the air. Brady stared at the dog. Grit tipped his head sideways and stared back.

Brady turned his eyes into laser beams. He concentrated.

Grit blinked.

Gotcha! thought Brady. He sighed. Grit wasn't so tough. He just thought he was tough.

I could make him like me, thought Brady bravely. I could do it if I had more time.

The dog show was in four days.

Time. He just needed time with Grit. Lots of time.

Forget it. He must be crazy.

The problem was, he was going to look so stupid. Everyone was expecting him to bring Grit. Champion Frisbee catcher. Six times. Why had he opened his big mouth?

Brady sucked in his breath. His words

poured out in a flood. "Mom, why don't I help Gramp in the daytime? Just while you're at work. Until you have time to hire a new housekeeper."

Mom's mouth fell open.

"It'd be fun." Brady's voice squeaked. Mom looked at him doubtfully. He forced himself to smile. "I could start tomorrow morning. It would be way better than going to the Rec Center."

Mom looked hurt. "I signed you up for puppets. And silk painting."

"I could do them next year," said Brady quickly. Puppets and silk painting? It would probably be full of girls. All the good stuff like soccer and swimming had been full when Brady and Mom checked into courses.

"Well," said Mom slowly. "The emergency numbers are by the phone. It would be mostly keeping Gramp company. And making sure he eats his lunch. I'm arranging Meals on Wheels for his dinners."

"I know all about the four food groups," said Brady. "And I can learn how to dust."

Mom smiled. "Well, why not? Why not? It would be a wonderful experience for both of you. Brady, you are being extremely thoughtful. Extremely."

Gramp slid open one eye. Brady gave him a smug look.

"You'll really get to know each other," said Mom.

"Anyone for poker?" said Gramp.

Brady groaned. What had he let himself in for?

chapter five

Gramp pulled back the curtain at the kitchen window. "It's your girlfriend."

"Very funny." Brady sank his hands into the warm soapy dishwater. He pulled the plug. Wobbly stacks of clean dishes sat in puddles along the counter. The floor looked like a swimming pool.

Gramp took a glass pickle jar off the top of the fridge. He unscrewed the lid and dug out a handful of crumpled bills. "As long as you're going out, you can get us some grub."

"Who said anything about going out?" Brady peeked around the edge of the curtain. Abra was hanging onto Gramp's gate, staring at the house. Cool It was leaping against the trunk of a tree and barking, his leash trailing on the ground. "Besides, Mom told me to heat up that leftover tuna casserole for lunch."

Brady and Gramp looked at each other. "Okay, okay," said Brady. "But you better write me a list. And don't tell Mom."

Grit wandered into the kitchen. He sloshed across the floor and slid under the table. Brady sucked in his breath. It was now or never. "Want to come, Grit? Good boy."

Grit stretched his lips back and yawned.

"Walkie, walkie," said Brady. His face felt hot.

Grit twisted himself into a pretzel. He burrowed his nose into his tummy and made snuffling noises.

"Fleas," said Brady.

Gramp handed Brady his list.

"I said, your dog has...oh, never mind."

Brady studied the list. Gramp's writing looked like spiderwebs. The grocery store was four blocks past Reptile Rage. He'd never be able to carry all those groceries on his bike. And the radio had predicted the hottest day of the summer so far. Brady thought about Desert Racer, waiting in the cool garage.

"I sure wouldn't mind a ride." He looked hopefully at Gramp. "Like in a truck or something."

Gramp snorted. "Kids don't walk these days. When I was a boy, I walked eight miles to school."

Brady groaned. Next would come the stories about all the wild horses Gramp broke and the million miles of fences he fixed. With a huge sigh he stuffed the money and grocery list into his pocket.

"You really should do something with that dog," he said.

Just before he slammed the door, he heard a low rumble from Grit. And a gleeful chuckle from Gramp.

"So where are we going?" said Abra.

Brady gave her a hard look. She had pulled her hair into one big pigtail that stuck out on the side of her head like a tap. At least it was a normal brown color today, and she had left her witch's hat at home.

He hesitated. Cool It danced in circles, looking hopeful. Brady took a couple of steps backwards. "Grocery shopping for Gramp. I guess you can come."

"Actually, you don't own the street," said Abra. "You can't own streets. And how come your grandfather doesn't ever come out?"

"He's...um...sick, all right?"

"What's the matter with him?"

Brady's shoulders tightened. On Jupiter, they probably didn't have girls. "You wouldn't understand."

He didn't really get it himself. Mom said Gramp never used to be this way. She said Gramp never stayed still a minute when Gramma was alive, between working with her on the ranch and taking Grit to dog competitions. And driving Desert Racer, Brady had thought silently. Even Mom didn't seem to know about Desert Racer. He sighed. You'd think Gramp would go nuts staying inside that gloomy old house day after day. But Brady had seen the frightened look in Gramp's eyes when Mom suggested once that they take a picnic supper to the park.

Abra was staring at him. Brady changed the subject. He eyed Cool It. "Is this dog trained yet?"

Abra smiled thinly. "Of course." She picked up the end of her dog's leash. "Come on, Cool It. Heel!"

They trudged along the hot sidewalk to the grocery store.

Abra smiled proudly at her dog. "I think Cool It's beginning to understa — "

Rooof! Cool It gave one gigantic leap forward. He yanked the leash out of Abra's hand and bounded off in pursuit of a sleek Siamese cat. Brady watched in horror as Cool It crashed into a flower bed and disappeared through an open gate. He cringed when he heard the crash of an overturned garbage can and a man's voice roaring in rage.

"Some trained dog," hissed Brady twenty minutes later, when he and Abra had picked up the last piece of sticky, smelly garbage strewn over the yard. Cool It lay in a shady patch, tied to the fence with his leash, watching with interest. He waved his tail enthusiastically when they set off again.

Brady hunched his shoulders and walked as fast as he could.

When they got to the grocery store, Abra said, "Maybe I should bring him inside."

"Bad idea," said Brady quickly. He frowned at Cool It. The dog's pink tongue hung out of the corner of his mouth. "Will he bark if we leave him out here?"

Abra tugged at her pigtail. "He might."

"Well, he can't come with us."

Brady watched while Abra tied the leash around a post. He stared at the panting dog. "Listen here, Cool It. Behave yourself. Down!"

Woof! Cool It flopped down on the pavement. He stared at Brady with his liquid eyes. Brady tried not to look shocked. He tried to look as if it were perfectly normal for a huge, slobbering, tail-crashing dog to obey him. He smiled weakly at Abra. "That's how you do it. You have to let your dog know who's boss."

"Oh really?" said Abra. "Julia wants to know how *your* dog training is coming along."

Brady ignored her. He grabbed a grocery cart and pushed it through the door. He cruised up and down the aisles, clutching Gramp's list. "Potato chips, wieners, cookies," he muttered as he filled the cart.

Abra trailed behind him. "This doesn't look very healthy. My mom would kill me if I bought all that junk."

Brady groaned. "Go get a bag of carrots if you're so worried."

Abra wandered off and came back a few minutes later with the carrots and a flyer. "They had these at the door. There's a special on tuna fish."

"Gramp hates tuna fish," said Brady. "So do I." He slid a case of orange pop onto the bottom rack of the cart. "Now, chocolate chunk ice cream and we can go."

When everything was paid for, they

went back outside. Cool It was lunging at the end of the leash, barking ecstatically at a lady with a poodle. The lady gave Brady and Abra a frozen look.

"Right," said Abra. "Just let him know who's boss."

Brady's cheeks burned. "You should train your dog better." He lifted the bags out of the cart. "Can you carry the small one? I've got one more stop."

Brady and Abra walked four more blocks to the library. Abra stayed outside with Cool It. Brady pushed through the door and hurried to the animal section. Frowning, he scanned the rows of books. *You Can be a Vet at Home. A Gerbil's Worst Nightmare. Make Money With Your Pet. Good Dog! Bad Dog!*

Brady glanced through the wide window at the front of the library. Abra was peering into one of the grocery bags. She looked worried. Brady slid *Good Dog! Bad Dog*! off the shelf. He examined the picture on the back cover. A big man with a black beard beamed. Dogs with lolling tongues and bright eyes crowded around him. Brady had a good feeling about this guy.

Brady sped to the checkout counter and signed out the book. He slid it under his T-shirt.

When he got outside, Abra said, "What did you get?"

"Nothing," said Brady. He wasn't going to tell Abra he was about to discover the secret to dog training. He leaned over the bag of groceries and slipped the book between the wieners and potato chips. He picked up the bag. "Okay, let's go."

Abra was staring at him oddly.

Brady shifted the bag to his other arm. "What?"

Abra grinned. "Nothing, except the ice cream's melting."

They both stared at the thin brown stream trickling down Brady's arm.

"Gramp and I like our ice cream soft," said Brady in an icy voice. He held his head high and marched down the sidewalk.

chapter six

Brady slid onto the front seat of Desert Racer. For a few minutes he forgot about the dog show. He couldn't believe his luck. Gramp must have forgotten all about locking the garage. Brady had seen trucks like Desert Racer on TV once. They crawled over boulders and skidded down gullies, their huge tires churning up the ground. Brady gripped the steering wheel. He could almost hear the crowd cheering and smell the dust.

In the distance, Cool It's tennis ball thumped against the fence. Abra's voice shouted, "Good dog, Cool it! Good dog!" Brady's stomach tightened. With a sigh he opened the book on his lap.

He'd finished the first three chapters of *Good Dog! Bad Dog!* last night in bed. They were mostly about looking after your dog, feeding it a proper diet and brushing it every day. There was a lot to this dog thing. Mom had finally made him turn out his light at eleven o'clock.

He read chapter four at breakfast. It was called "Dog First Aid" and had a disgusting picture of someone giving mouth-to-mouth resuscitation to a dog. Brady was so absorbed he barely heard Mom's final instructions. "Remember to wear your bike helmet. Give Gramp his pills just before lunch. I'll pick up pizza and bring it by for supper."

When Brady got to Gramp's house, he had washed Gramp's breakfast dishes and played ten games of Hearts. Finally, exhausted by all his victories, Gramp had slumped back in his chair and fallen asleep. Brady had slipped out to the garage.

Brady wasn't sure how long he'd been sitting in Gramp's truck. He fought back a growing sense of panic. Only two days left until the dog show and he was getting nowhere. He studied the title of chapter five and felt a tiny twinge of hope. "Keys to Communication."

Brady read slowly. *Dogs talk with their voices and their actions. Dogs who are friends greet each other in a typical manner. They sniff each other from head to tail. Sometimes a dog will hold its paw up, or stick its rump in the air and wag its tail. A happy dog smiles with its mouth open and its tongue lolling. This is dog talk.*

Dog talk. Brady had never heard of that before. He leaned back against the seat and frowned.

Dog talk.

He reread the line, *Dogs who are friends greet each other in a typical manner.*

He thought hard. Maybe, just maybe, he'd been doing this all wrong. He'd been afraid of Grit, and Grit knew it.

"Inside, Grit is just a friendly old mutt," said Brady in a loud voice. He said it ten more times.

He shut the book with a bang. Dog talk. He could try. He was desperate enough to try anything. He hurried back to the house. Water was running in the bathroom, and Gramp's wobbly voice was singing "Home on the Range." The coast was clear.

It didn't take a lot of brains to figure out where Grit was. Brady crouched down on his hands and knees and crawled into the kitchen. Grit watched in surprise from under the table.

"Woof!" said Brady in a soft voice. "Woof!"

He inched closer to the table. "Inside, you are just a friendly old mutt," he said. He crept in a slow circle around Grit. He took a deep breath and put his face next to Grit's neck.

Nothing happened.

Brady's shoulders relaxed. Now for part two. He sniffed.

Sniff, sniff, sniff.

Cautiously, he sniffed his way down

to Grit's tail. Grit twisted his neck to see what Brady was doing.

So far, so good. Grit was definitely interested. In fact, he looked astonished. Brady backed off a bit and lifted his arm. He curled his hand over like a paw.

"Woof! Woof!" he barked.

Dog talk.

Grit pricked his ears.

"Now!" muttered Brady. He stuck out his rear end and wiggled. He opened his mouth and hung his tongue out the side. He gave Grit one big happy dog grin.

Hoooo, howled Grit. His eyes rolled in his head. He scrabbled to his feet, nails screeching on the linoleum.

"Help!" screamed Brady, diving out of the way.

Gramp padded into the kitchen, wrapped in an orange bath towel. Water dripped in a pool around his feet.

Rrroooow! Grit dove between Gramp's legs. He skidded on the wet floor and sailed on his rump through the doorway.

Hooooo. He gathered himself up and skittered down the hallway.

Brady stood up. His legs shook like Jell-O. He gave Gramp his best doggy smile. "It must be my dog breath," he said weakly.

Then he bolted outside.

chapter seven

Brady ran all the way to Reptile Rage.

Only Dextra was there, cleaning out a litter box in the front window. She was wearing a Save the Rhinos T-shirt. She smiled at Brady. "Can I help you with anything?"

Brady took a deep breath. "Uh...you know your dog show? On Friday? I thought it would be a good idea to postpone it for a while. So more kids can hear about it."

"Oh, you don't have to worry about that," said Dextra. "I think the whole town knows. We've got tons of entries!"

Brady sighed. "I might be on Jupiter."

The bell over the front door jingled. A woman dragged a little boy with a melting purple Popsicle into the store. Dextra looked at Brady. "Is there anything else?"

"Uh, yeah," said Brady quickly. "Do you have anything that's guaranteed to drive a dog crazy? Special treats or something." He made his voice sound like a TV commercial. "Feed your dog this, and you'll have a friend for life."

Dextra frowned. "We discourage spoiling dogs with lots of treats. Treats are no substitute for consistent, firm, fair training."

"I agree," said Brady. "Absolutely. Think of this as a...reward. For excellent behavior."

"In that case, you might try Doggie Delights. We sell them in bulk in that barrel over there. Dogs do love them."

The Doggie Delights looked like round brown cookies. Brady sniffed one. Not bad.

Brady waited while the boy with

the Popsicle chose between a catnip mouse and a ball that squeaked when you squished it. Finally the mother gave in and bought both. Brady paid for a whole bag of Doggie Delights. He raced back to Gramp's house.

Abra and Julia were sitting on the porch stairs. Abra was reading *Good Dog! Bad Dog!*

"Hey! What do you think you're doing? Where'd you get that?"

Abra dropped the book. "You left it out here. Can we come in and see your grandfather?"

"No. Look, why can't you just leave us alone?"

Julia made her eyes like slits. "Where's your dog?"

"He's in the house. He's having a rest in between training sessions." Brady reached into his bag. "Look, I'll give you some cookies if you don't bug me."

"Oh yuck, boy cookies," said Julia.

"Gingersnaps," said Brady. He waved one in the air.

"Okay," said Abra. "I'm hungry."

Brady handed Abra two Doggie

Delights. "Now leave me alone."

Gramp was asleep in the armchair in the living room. Grit sprawled across his feet. His eyebrows wrinkled when he saw Brady.

"Keep your shirt on," muttered Brady. He waved his bag of treats. "You are about to enter Dog Heaven."

He took a cookie out of the bag. He dangled it in front of Grit's nose.

Whump! Grit grabbed it and swallowed it in one gulp. Brady peered at Gramp's face. His mouth hung open. He was snoring softly.

"Good going, Grit," whispered Brady. His heart thumped. He gave Grit two more cookies. The dog wiggled his rear end. His tongue lolled.

Dog talk! Grit was smiling. He loved this. He loved Brady.

Brady took a deep breath. "Okay, buddy, there's lots more where those came from. But you gotta do something for me. A walk. One measly little walk. Deal?"

Grit whined.

"Come on, that's fair."

Brady slipped his hands under the red bandana. He pulled.

Grit whined harder.

Brady pulled harder. "Walkie, walkie," he said.

He felt Grit's cold teeth on his hand.

"YEOW!" Brady leaped up. He danced around in a circle. "WHAT DO YOU THINK YOU'RE DOING?" he shouted.

Grit dove under Gramp's chair. *Hoooo.*

Gramp sat bolt upright. "It's a stampede!" he hollered.

"Your dog is a killer!" Brady shouted back.

Brady showed Gramp his wound. If you looked really hard, you could almost see blood.

Gramp hummed cheerfully. He took Brady into the bathroom and poured something from a dusty brown bottle over his hand. "Horse liniment," he said gleefully. "It'll cure you or kill you."

Brady stuck five Band-Aids on his hand and wandered outside. He slumped on the step and closed his eyes. He had run out of ideas.

The gate squeaked. "Hey!" said Abra's voice. Brady opened his eyes.

Abra stared at his bandages. "What did you do to your hand?"

Brady frowned. "I stuck it in the garburator."

"Actually, old houses don't have garburators." Abra stood on one foot. "Do you have any more of those cookies?"

"What?" Brady blinked at her.

Abra shrugged. "They weren't bad."

"Wait a sec," said Brady. He went inside and got the bag of Doggie Delights. He watched while Abra bit into one.

He took one out of the bag and studied it for a minute. Doggie Delights. What a flop. He took a tiny nibble on the edge.

It was crunchy. And it tasted a bit like cinnamon. With a sigh he finished it and reached for another one.

Dog training had made him hungry.

chapter eight

Whoosh!

A coil of rope flew across the kitchen. It landed with a thump around Brady's shoulders.

Gramp popped through the doorway. He wore a black cowboy hat and boots with high heels and pointy toes. "Gotcha!"

"Hey!" sputtered Brady. He tugged at the rope. "What do you think you're doing?"

"Ropin' you!" said Gramp. "Ha! You're an ornery cow. Might have to throw you down and hog-tie you!"

"Very funny." Brady wriggled and the rope pulled harder. "Would you mind getting this thing off me?"

"If you promise to play Crazy Eights."

"I'm playing with my race car." Brady had laid out an imaginary racetrack on the patterned squares of linoleum. For a few minutes he'd forgotten about Grit and the dog show.

Gramp jiggled the rope. "Crazy Eights."

Brady's shoulders sagged. "Okay, okay." He glared at Gramp. He was the one who was crazy.

Gramp untied Brady. He coiled his rope and slung it over a chair. "I'll be waiting for you. Bring us some grub while you're at it."

Brady grabbed a bag of potato chips, some cookies and four cans of orange pop and carried the food into the living room. He slid deeper in his chair as Gramp skunked him, game after game. It was hard to concentrate on the cards. His mind drifted to Desert Racer. He'd love to ask Gramp a million questions. How fast could it go? Had he ever won a race in it? And why was it such a secret anyway?

Brady sighed. He couldn't think of a way to bring it up without making Gramp suspicious. He drained two cans of pop. Then he said, "I quit."

Gramp crunched a potato chip. "Can't. We're playing best out of twenty-five."

"What?" Brady's voice shot up.

Gramp stuck out his chin. Grit growled softly at his feet. Brady rubbed his hands through his hair. "Look, as soon as I win one game, we quit."

Gramp snickered. He dealt a new round. His fingers looked like old tree roots, but they moved as fast as spiders. Brady checked his cards gloomily.

They played for a few minutes. *Slap, slap* went the cards. Brady felt horrible. He'd had way too much orange pop. He sneezed. "I think I'm allergic to the dust in here."

Gramp snorted. "You're the housekeeper." He slapped his final card down. "Skunked!" He made a tally mark on a piece of paper. His side of the paper was filled with tally marks. Gramp took a slurp of pop. "Yee-haw!"

Brady hated it when Gramp used his dumb cowboy talk. Cowboys probably never even said yee-haw. He leaned over and fiddled with his shoelace. He'd heard somewhere that hanging your head upside down made you smarter. It had something to do with the blood rushing to your brain. Maybe it made you luckier too. Grit watched Brady, his chin resting on the floor. Brady stuck out his tongue. Grit curled back his lip.

Zzzz, zzzz, zzzzz. Brady beamed a potato chip laser gun at Grit's head. Got him!

Gramp banged his can on the table. "Get into the game, boy!"

"Brady, the name is Brady." Brady sat up slowly. Instead of feeling luckier, he felt sicker. His eyes flickered over the photo of Grit in the gold frame on the wall behind Gramp. It looked as if Grit was staring right at him and laughing. Brady's stomach felt hollow.

In the next round, Gramp slapped

an eight of spades on the pile. He peered slyly at Brady. "I change it to diamonds."

Brady blinked. He stared at his cards. An eight of hearts. And the rest were diamonds. Brady looked back at the pile of cards on the table. Then at his hand. I can win this, he thought.

Brady stood up. "I'll just be a sec. I need some water." On the way to the kitchen, he walked behind Gramp's chair. He peeked at his cards. No eights.

Brady took his time in the kitchen. He splashed cold water on his face and stuck his mouth under the tap for a drink. When he got back, Gramp was hunched over the cards. His cheeks were pink. His gray hair stuck up like an owl.

Whack, whack, whack! They banged the cards on the table.

"Ready for the kill," murmured Brady. He stared at his last diamond.

Gramp threw down an eight of clubs. "Changing it to spades. Gotcha, boy!"

"NO WAY!" Brady's head pounded. He jumped to his feet. "Where did you get that eight?"

Brady knew he was shouting, but he didn't care. He swiped his hands through the cards. "You're a cheater. You probably cheated in every game."

Gramp's eyes popped out. "I did not!"

"You did too! That's how you keep winning. You're nothing but a crazy old cheater."

Brady's head swam. Sweat prickled the back of his neck. "And my name is BRADY," he gasped. Then, with a huge shudder, he threw up all over the scattered cards.

chapter nine

Brady filled the bathroom sink with cold water. He dunked his head. He shook like a dog. Water drops splattered on the mirror.

"Grrr...," growled Brady. He waggled his tongue and rolled his eyes. "Watch out! I have rabies!"

Brady wiped his face and arms with a towel and slipped down the hallway, past Gramp's bedroom. The door was partly open. Gramp perched on the edge of his bed. Grit sat in front of him, resting his silky head on Gramp's knees.

For a second Brady felt guilty when

he thought of the ruined card game. Gramp had made a big deal about searching for a bucket and a mop to clean it up. Then he remembered what Gramp had done. It serves him right, thought Brady. Gramp was nothing but a crazy old cheater. With a mean, old, used-up dog.

Brady slid out the front door and shut it quietly behind him. He leaned on the porch railing. Abra was playing in her front yard with Cool It. She threw an old green tennis ball against the side of her house. It bounced back and rolled between Cool It's front legs. He pounced on it and tore around the yard in a wild circle.

"The incredible, the amazing, the unbelievable SUPER DOG," she said in a piercing voice. She gave a low bow. "And now, SUPER DOG will..."

Brady jumped off the porch and stuck his head over the fence. "How's your training going?"

"Great." Abra and Brady stared at Cool It. He had dropped the tennis ball and was digging frantically in a corner of a flower bed.

Abra sighed. "Awful, actually. I can't believe the show is tomorrow. I wish I'd never heard of it."

"Me too," said Brady.

Cool It abandoned his hole and bounded over to Abra. He planted his dirty paws in the middle of her T-shirt and grinned.

Abra and Brady laughed. Brady wondered how he had ever been afraid of Cool It. He was just a big mush. Abra pushed her dog away. "Do you want some lemonade?"

Brady hesitated. So far, Abra hadn't said one thing about his dog training or Gramp. And he *was* hot. "Okay."

The kitchen in Abra's house was bright. Pots brimming with red flowers filled the windowsill. Abra's mother was checking something in the oven. Brady's stomach rumbled. It smelled delicious.

Abra's mother smiled. "Hi, I'm Sue. You must be Brady. Abra told me you're staying with your grandfather."

"Just in the day," said Brady. "I'm

helping out until Mom finds a new housekeeper. She can't do it because she started her new job."

"Well, you must be a very thoughtful boy. I've been meaning to take something over for your grandfather, but I've been awfully busy getting the house straightened around since we got back. I'll try to get a casserole put together."

Resentment flooded through Brady's head. He thought about all the times Gramp had skunked him in cards. He thought about Gramp's gloating face. He thought about Grit. "Tuna," he said. "Maybe you could make a whole bunch of tuna fish casseroles, and he could freeze them and eat them all winter."

Sue and Brady beamed at each other. Then Abra said, "Brady caught his hand in the garburator."

Brady's cheeks burned. "I do the cooking and stuff over there," he mumbled.

"Oh," said Sue. She frowned. "That's a lot of responsibility for a young boy."

"It's okay," said Brady. "We mostly eat hot dogs and chips."

Sue's frown deepened.

"Sometimes he gets locked in the attic," said Abra.

Sue stared at Brady. "Good heavens!"

Brady wiggled. "Actually..."

"You poor boy! Abra, I want you to lay an extra place at the table. We're having Chicken Supreme for lunch, and it's almost ready." She patted Brady's head. "And then we'll see about all this. Where did you say your mother was working?"

"The credit union."

Brady plopped into a chair with a huge sigh. Chicken Supreme. It smelled almost as good as Mom's. And he was starving.

chapter ten

"Grit, ask the boy to pass the ketchup," said Gramp.

Brady sighed. Gramp was still sore about the ruined cards. He shoved the ketchup bottle across the table. Gramp poured ketchup along a wiener. He broke his hot dog in half and slid one piece under the table.

"It's not healthy for dogs..." Brady started to say. Then he changed his mind. He pushed his hot dog across his plate. He was still full of Chicken Supreme.

"Grit, ask the boy for the mustard."

Brady groaned. A car door slammed. He jumped up and peered out the window hopefully. Maybe Mom was early.

A woman who looked like Julia was marching up the walk. She was armed with a mop and a broom and a bucket. Abra's mom, Sue, followed her, carrying a huge casserole dish.

Brady glanced uneasily at Gramp. Then he sped to the front door to block them. They swept past.

"This is dreadful," said Sue.

"A fire trap," said Julia's mother.

Sue carried her dish into the kitchen. "Tuna fish casserole. You'll need to preheat the oven to 375 degrees and warm the casserole for forty-five minutes. Take the foil off for the last ten to brown the top."

"Now," said Julia's mother. "Let's get to work."

Brady looked around wildly. Gramp had disappeared like a wisp of smoke. Sue was sweeping the kitchen floor vigorously. Dust balls whirled in the air. Julia's mother opened Gramp's cupboards. She said, "Oh my." She

produced a clipboard and a pencil from a bag and began writing.

"Hey," said Brady. His voice cracked. "You can't do this."

He backed into the living room. Sue charged after him. She pulled the curtains wide open. The bright light blinded Brady. He ran into the hallway. Gramp fluttered in the shadows like a bird. Grit circled his legs and whined.

"Gramp, do something," hissed Brady. "Get your rope and hog-tie them. It's *your* house."

Gramp opened and shut his mouth. Sue walked past, dragging an old dusty saddle. Gramp moaned and disappeared into his bedroom.

"Look," said Brady. "I mean really ... don't you think..." He gulped as Sue came by a second time with one of the broken TVs.

"It's looking better in here already," said Sue brightly. "Thank goodness you alerted us, Brady."

Brady gave up. He went upstairs and flipped through Gramp's comics, trying to drown out the sounds of cleaning. He thought about the time Mom cleaned his bedroom while he was away at Beaver camp. She'd thrown away the cat skull he'd found in the dumpster and his half-rotten crab. She'd sorted through his cupboards and put stuff in boxes with labels. Brady shuddered. He had never totally forgiven her.

When the house was quiet, Brady crept downstairs. The smell of floor wax and disinfectant stung his nose. The floors were so shiny they were dangerous. A note on the kitchen counter said, *Casserole in fridge. 375 degrees. 45 minutes.*

Forty-five minutes was a long time. Gramp was probably starving, since he hadn't had a chance to finish his hot dog. Brady turned the oven to five hundred. He stuck the casserole on the top rack.

The phone rang. Brady picked it up on the third ring. It was Mom. "Brady," she said, "what's going on?"

"Nothing," said Brady. "Nothing's going on." He could hear breathing in the background.

Mom could hear it too. "Dad, is that you on the other phone?"

"Yes," said Gramp sulkily.

"Good. Now I've got the two of you on here, I want you both to listen carefully. Do you understand?"

"Yes," said Gramp and Brady.

"First of all, Dad, I hope you're not gloating over your card games."

"No, dear," said Gramp.

"And Brady, I got the strangest call at my office a little while ago from Gramp's neighbor. She said she was Abra's mother. Some nonsense about garburators and attics."

Brady was silent.

"Gramp's house doesn't have a garburator," said Mom. "Can't you find something constructive to do with that imagination of yours?"

Brady sighed. "Yes, Mom."

"Honestly, you and Gramp are two peas in a pod!"

After Mom hung up, Brady stayed on the line. "Uh, Gramp? Why don't you come out now? Those women are gone. There's... uh... some kind of casserole in the oven." He paused. "I could scrunch up potato chips to put on top."

Brady set the phone down gently. He laid two places at the kitchen table. He cut up some carrots and put them on a plate.

"It smells burnt," said Gramp from the doorway. He was wearing his bear paw slippers and his galloping horse pajamas. "I hate burnt tuna fish casserole."

Brady opened the oven door. He put potato chips on the burnt bits. Then he dished it up.

He peeked at Gramp. Gramp was piling the pieces of celery in a wobbly hill. Gramp hated celery and tidy rooms, just like Brady. He loved orange pop and comic books and collecting junk. Maybe that's what Mom meant when she said they were two peas in a pod.

Brady took a deep breath.

"Gramp," he said, "I have a big problem."

chapter eleven

"Come on," said Gramp. "I want to show you something. Before your mother gets here."

Brady pushed back his chair from the kitchen table. His head was buzzing with Gramp's plan. They'd been working out the details for an hour. It was perfect. It would save Brady's life. If only he had the nerve to do it.

"We'll go out the back way," said Gramp.

Brady thought Gramp was joking. Then, with growing excitement, he followed Gramp out the back door. Gramp glanced from side to side like a nervous cat as he led Brady through the long grass to the old garage.

Gramp looked at Brady sideways, and for a second Brady thought he winked. "Can't seem to remember to keep this door locked." He pushed it open. Desert Racer gleamed in the shaft of sunlight. "What do you think?"

Brady bit his lip. He wanted to be honest. "I've seen it before."

"Well, I know that," said Gramp impatiently. "I said, what do you think?"

"I think it's...the best racing truck in the whole world. The galaxy. Maybe even the universe."

"Huh," grunted Gramp. "Get in."

He and Brady sat side by side on the front seat. Gramp showed Brady how the controls worked.

"Did you ever race it?" said Brady.

"'Course," said Gramp. "The Desert Classic 500. Finished the whole course and came in third."

"Wow." Brady let this sink in. "Did Gramma know about this?"

"Nope."

"Mom?"

"Nope." Gramp looked sideways at Brady. "They'd have worried, see? Said I was too old or some nonsense."

Brady nodded. Mothers and grandmothers were like that. He had a thousand more questions to ask Gramp. Like, would he ever drive it again? But something in Gramp's face stopped him. They sat in silence for a long time. Then Gramp said, "We better go get that dog of yours ready."

Brady's mind shifted back to the dog show. What if the plan flopped? The kids would think he was nuts. Brady shivered. He was scared. But excited too.

Brady's cowboy boots clicked on the sidewalk. He carried a cardboard carton. All night, Gramp's last-minute instructions had tumbled through his mind. Dextra had set up a long table in the parking lot behind the pet store. Ropes and orange pylons marked off a large circle. Brady shifted the box in his arms. He noticed a red pickup truck with the words "Reptile Rage" printed on the sides. "Is it okay if I leave something in the back of your truck?" he asked Dextra. "It's for the show."

"Sure. And since you're the first one here, how about sorting out these ribbons for me?"

The ribbons were blue with gold lettering. Each one was attached to a cardboard tag with the category and a place for the dog's and the owner's names. They were twice as big as the ribbons at sports day at school. Brady laid them on the table in a neat row so the categories showed. His stomach felt hollow, and his heart thudded. The plan had seemed perfect when he and Gramp thought it up. Now he wasn't so sure.

Dextra gave him a card with the number one on it. He pinned it to his shirt. He printed his name on a piece of paper on her clipboard. His hands felt clammy.

"Good luck," said Dextra.

"I'll need it," mumbled Brady. He

watched the other kids arrive with their dogs. There were huge ones and tiny ones. Some had stripes, and some had spots. Brady identified a chocolate lab, a cocker spaniel with floppy ears and a poodle with a pink bow. The parking lot filled with growls and shrill barks and excited voices.

Brady waved at Abra. He walked over to pat Cool It, who strained at his leash.

"I think I'm going to be sick," said Abra.

"Everyone signed up?" Dextra shouted into a megaphone. "Okay, let's get started."

Brady hurried over to her side. His forehead prickled with sweat. "Can I go last?" he whispered.

Dextra nodded and called number two. A tall German Shepherd with a glossy coat and bright eyes bounded into the ring. A boy with red hair said firmly, "Heel!" and the dog moved obediently to his side.

The boy said, "Sit." The dog dropped to his haunches, his head tilted proudly.

Abra nudged Cool It. "I hope you're watching this. You might learn something."

Dextra moved through the numbers quickly. When it was Abra's turn, Brady's chest tightened. Abra tugged Cool It around in a circle. She started to say, "The incredible, the amazing, the..." She stopped and sighed. "Oh, never mind." She took the green tennis ball out of her pocket and threw it. "Fetch!"

The ball shot past a pylon and between a girl's legs. Cool It dove into the crowd. After a minute he returned with a pop can in his mouth. Abra's face was as red as a strawberry, but everyone clapped and cheered. Brady cheered the loudest. It was a great trick.

"We have one more entry," said Dextra. She had been laughing so hard, she was crying. "And then we'll hand out the ribbons."

Brady walked over to the truck. His heart leaped around in his chest like a Ping-Pong ball. His legs felt like cement. He could feel everyone's eyes burning into his back.

Slowly, he walked back to the circle.

Bump, bump, bump, went something behind his legs.

Brady took a deep breath. "Meet Log the Dog."

The only sound was his heart thumping like crazy. He dragged a log, tied to the end of a long yellow rope, around the pylons. He had tied a blue bandana around one end of the log. Abra's eyes were huge. Julia poked her arm and whispered furiously.

Brady wanted to sink into the parking lot and disappear. But he heard himself say, "This is Log. He's the easiest kind of dog to look after. He doesn't eat much, and he sleeps a lot."

The boy with the German Shepherd snickered. Brady's face felt like it was on fire. He talked faster. "Log is very well trained. He can roll over..." He nudged the log with his foot, and it rolled across the pavement.

Someone clapped, and a lot of kids laughed. Brady sneaked a glance at Abra. She was grinning from ear to ear.

"And if I say STAY, he never budges."

Everyone was laughing now. The sick feeling evaporated. Brady laughed too. He dragged Log around the circle one last time. He finished by saying, "If your parents won't let you get a dog because they bark too much, this is the dog for you!"

Dextra wiped her eyes and handed out the ribbons. Everybody got one. Cool It got *Most Enthusiastic*. Popsicle got *Best Groomed*. And Log got *Most Original*.

"That was a great idea," said a voice behind Brady. He spun around. It was one of the boys from the park.

Brady grinned. "Thanks!"

Everyone around him was talking. Brady's shoulders relaxed. This town wasn't so bad after all. Maybe some of these guys would be interested in building the space station. He'd even ask Abra. She was pretty nice for a girl. Actually, she was great.

But first, Brady had something important to do.

"I'll see you guys later!" he said. He raced down the street to Gramp's

house, dragging Log the Dog behind him. He couldn't wait to show Gramp the ribbon.

He leaped up the porch steps. "Gramp!"

The house was quiet. The smell of floor polish lingered in the air.

"Gramp! Grit! Where are you?"

A cold prickle crept up his back. The house was empty. But Gramp never went out. Never.

So where could he be?

chapter twelve

"Gramp never goes out," Brady said for the hundredth time. "Something must have happened."

Abra chewed her nail. "It's hard for me to help find him when I've hardly ever seen him. I need a description."

"What? He looks... old! How many other old people do you think are going to be wandering around?"

Brady tried to remember if Gramp had been dressed when he'd left for the dog show. "He might be wearing pajamas with wild horses on them. And slippers that look like bear paws."

Abra's eyes widened. "Maybe you could get something that belongs to him from the house. We could give it to Cool It to smell, and he could track him down."

"Great idea!" Brady shot into the house and grabbed a boot out of the hall cupboard. He waved it in front of Cool It's nose. Cool It flapped his tail. He pricked his ears.

"Find Gramp!" shouted Abra.

Cool It charged around the block with Abra and Brady pounding at his heels. They ended up back at Gramp's gate. Cool It wagged his tail and collapsed panting on his tummy.

Brady hopped on one foot. The cowboy boots had given him a blister. "This is terrible!"

"I could ask Mom to help," said Abra doubtfully.

"No!" said Brady quickly. He had a terrifying vision of Sue and Julia's mother scouring the neighborhood, beating back bushes with their brooms. Gramp would hate that.

Brady had a sudden idea.

He hobbled through the long grass behind the house to the garage. The two wide doors at the back hung open. Brady stared into the empty garage.

"Desert Racer is gone!" he shouted.

He and Abra trudged back to the front of the house. They sat with slumped shoulders on the porch steps. Brady's head ached. Desert Racer probably hadn't been out of the garage for years. The engine could overheat. It could run out of gas. Its tires could explode. Gramp could be in big trouble. Brady groaned. He leaned his head against the side of the house and shut his eyes.

Suddenly he heard a loud roar and a squeal of tires. Brady's eyes popped open. Desert Racer lurched to a stop in front of the house. The yellow lightning bolts gleamed in the sun, and the flames of fire licking the hood looked alive. Gramp clutched the steering wheel, his black cowboy hat pulled low over his eyes. Grit stood up in the back and barked wildly.

"Yee-haw!" yelled Gramp. He turned and grinned gleefully at Brady. "That was the test drive! Hurry and get in! We don't have all day!"

Brady and Abra scrambled onto the seat beside Gramp. Gramp stepped on the accelerator and the truck shot forward.

"Where are we going?" yelled Brady over the roar of the engine.

"Don't disturb me!" Gramp hollered back. "I'm concentratin' on my drivin'!"

Brady leaned his head back. The air blew through the open windshield against his hot cheeks. He wished the kids from school could see him now. He grinned at Abra and she grinned back.

They drove past Reptile Rage and the grocery store and the library and onto the main road out of town. In a few minutes the houses were replaced by fields and scattered farms.

Gramp sucked in big breaths of air. He chuckled happily. Then he slowed down and stopped at the side of the road beside a stretch of barbed wire fence. "Get the gate, Brady," he said.

Brady hopped out of the truck and struggled with the floppy gate. Gramp

drove slowly into the bumpy field. Brady shut the gate carefully and leaped back in beside Abra. He looked worriedly at the farmhouse in the distance. "Gramp, do you know these people?"

"Hooo-eee!" shouted Gramp.

Desert Racer shot across the field. It bounced over ruts and mounds and lunged through dips. For a second Brady could see nothing but bright blue sky and then golden grass. He gripped the edge of the seat. Grit barked excitedly behind them.

"Hang on, Grit!" yelled Gramp as Desert Racer leaped over a rut. "Yee-haw! We're getting air!"

"Yee-haw!" Brady shouted back. He glanced over his shoulder. Grit's ears were sticking straight out at the sides and his mouth was open in a wide doggy grin. "Grit loves this!" he said.

"'Course he does!" Gramp grunted as the truck bounced in the air. "I put an anti-skid mat back there for him!"

Brady laughed out loud.

Desert Racer was better, way better than he'd ever imagined.

The farmhouse was getting closer and closer. For a terrible minute Brady thought Gramp was going to drive right into the side. But Gramp stepped hard on the brake, and Desert Racer bounced to a stop in the front yard.

Brady's head whirled as he waited for the dust to settle. He hoped the farmer wouldn't be angry. He climbed out of the truck. His legs felt wobbly and the ground was spinning.

A woman wearing an apron stood in the doorway of the farmhouse. She was smiling. A mass of furry black-and-white bodies squeezed past her legs and tumbled into the yard.

"Puppies!" said Abra.

Brady's heart gave a sharp jump. He couldn't stop staring at the puppies, which was dumb because he didn't even like dogs.

He stepped forward. One of the puppies pounced on a stick and wrestled it to the ground. Then he saw Brady and wiggled towards him, sniffing curiously. He had black-and-white fur and a rusty patch between his ears like Grit. He grabbed Brady's shoelace and tugged, growling deep in his throat.

"They're Grit's nieces and nephews," said Gramp.

Brady stooped down and picked up the puppy. It felt warm and surprisingly heavy in his arms.

"Your mom said you can have one." Gramp scratched Grit's ears busily and didn't look at Brady.

"No thanks," said Brady quickly. "I don't like dogs."

"Well, if you did want one, you know how to pick 'em," said Gramp. "That one you got there has all the makings of a Frisbee-catching champion."

"It does?" Brady made his voice sound casual.

Gramp squinted at the puppy. "Those long legs are a dead giveaway."

Brady tried to examine the wiggling ball of puppy in his arms. It looked like all fat body and fur to him. And sparkling brown eyes.

Brady sucked in his breath. His heart was thumping so hard he was sure Gramp could hear it.

Which was dumb because he didn't even like dogs.

"Just say I wanted this dog — would you help me train him?" said Brady. "I mean, to catch Frisbees and stuff?"

"Of course I would. But a dog needs a name first. A real good name. You got to take your time when you pick a name."

Brady nodded. His throat felt too thick to speak. But he didn't need to take his time. He knew already. He laughed as a warm pink tongue swiped his hand. Inside his head he whispered his puppy's name softly.

Jupiter.